# SAVE THE SHIELDON

## Based on the Episode "Ill-Will Hunting"

ADAPTED BY
SIMCHA WHITEHILL

**SCHOLASTIC INC.**

New York    Toronto    London    Auckland    Sydney
Mexico City    New Delhi    Hong Kong    Buenos Aires

ISBN-13: 978-0-545-07305-9
ISBN-10: 0-545-07305-7

Published by Scholastic Inc.
SCHOLASTIC and associated logos are trademarks and/or registered trademarks of Scholastic Inc.
Lexile is a registered trademark of MetaMetrics, Inc.

12 11 10 9 8 7 6 5 4 3 2 1      8 9 10 11 12/0

Designed by Henry Ng
Printed in the U.S.A.
First printing, September 2008

Pikachu pointed out some
wild Shieldon.
"How cute!" said Dawn.
"Pika-pika!" said Pikachu.

A big gray tank drove up.
"Oh no!" Brock yelled.
Goons were trying to steal
the Shieldon. They were sent
by Pokémon Hunter J.

Pikachu tried to scare them off. But Golbat hit the yellow Pokémon with Wing Attack.

Gary arrived with Electivire.
Zap! It shocked the goons
away.

"Hi Gary! You came just in time," Brock said.
Gary Oak was protecting all the Pokémon at Mt. Coronet.

"Wow! You are Professor Oak's grandson?" Dawn asks. "Yup! Nice to meet you, Dawn," Gary said.

Gary called Professor Rowan
for backup. He wanted to
move the Shieldon to a safe
place.

"We will help you!" Ash said.
They headed down the road
together.

Hunter J's goons found them again!

Ash wanted to battle them. Gary was worried the Shieldon might get hurt.

But they had no other choice.

Blastoise used Water Gun.
Pikachu used ThunderShock.
Umbreon used Sand-Attack.

But nothing could stop the goons.

Then, a bunch of wild Beedrill swooped in.

*Buzzzzzzzz!*

All the goons ran for cover behind some bushes.

Gary wanted to keep the Shieldon safe. But Ash wanted to battle the goons again.

"Cool it, Ash!" said Brock.
Brock and Dawn agreed with
Gary. They wanted to sneak
away with the Shieldon.
Ash listened to his friends.

"How are we going to get to Professor Rowan now?" Dawn asked.

The goons were still blocking the road.

"We'll have to go another way," Gary said.

He led them to a rocky mountain path.

A Shieldon slipped and fell.
"Shieldon-on-on!" Its
scream echoed in the canyon.

Together, they pulled it back
onto the path.
    "That was a close one!"
Brock said.

"Uh oh, here comes more trouble!" said Dawn.
  Hunter J swooped in on her Salamence. The goons arrived in their gray tank.

"Pikachu, use Iron Tail to distract them!" Ash said.

"Pikaaaaaa!" Pikachu yelled.

"Now run! Save the
Shieldon!" Ash yelled.
    Brock and Dawn took the
Pokémon up the mountain.
Gary stayed to help Ash battle.

Hunter J called on Drapion.
It attacked with Poison Tail.
Gary used Blastoise to
battle Salamence.

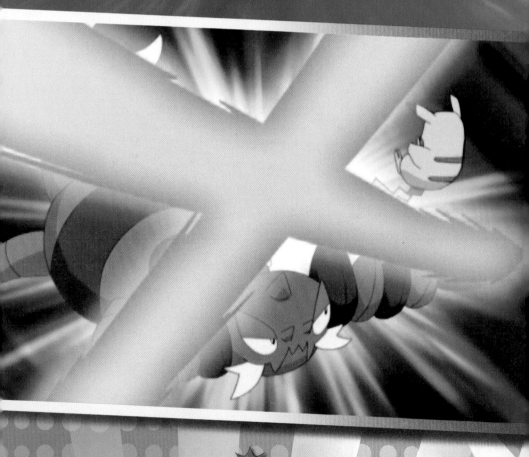

A Shieldon slid down the mountain.
"No, Shieldon!" Dawn cried.

*Pow!* Hunter J froze it.
Hunter J hopped on
Salamence and flew away.

Professor Rowan and Officer
Jenny arrived. Brock told them
what happened.
"We have to go after Hunter
J!" Officer Jenny said.

Ash and Gary followed the goons. They hid under their tank.

They arrived at Hunter J's
hideout. A bad guy was coming
to buy Shieldon.
    Ash sent Staravia to find
the others.

Gary and Ash snuck into the hideout.

Electivire, Umbreon, and Pikachu combined their attacks.

*Bam!* They blasted through the whole place.

Ash found Shieldon and
unfroze it.
Ash gave Shieldon a hug.

The bad buyer flew in on his helicopter. He could see Officer Jenny close by.
"I am out of here!" he said.

"Let's go before Officer Jenny catches us!" Hunter J yelled.

She and her goons ran away.

Officer Jenny pulled up with Professor Rowan. They were glad the Shieldon were safe. Gary said, "It is all thanks to Ash!"

"We did it together," said
Ash.
Gary and Ash shook hands.
"Best friends till the end!"
Gary said.